The Stranger Child

By

E. T. A. Hoffmann

British Library Cataloguing-in-Publication Data
A catalogue record for this book is available from the
British Library

Contents

E. T. A. Hoffman

Ernst Theodor Wilhelm Hoffmann was born in Königsberg, East Prussia in 1776. His family were all jurists, and during his youth he was initially encouraged to pursue a career in law. However, in his late teens Hoffman became increasingly interested in literature and philosophy, and spent much of his time reading German classicists and attending lectures by, amongst others, Immanuel Kant.

In was in his twenties, upon moving with his uncle to Berlin, that Hoffman first began to promote himself as a composer, writing an operetta called Die Maske and entering a number of playwriting competitions. Hoffman struggled to establish himself anywhere for a while, flitting between a number of cities and dodging the attentions of Napoleon's occupying troops. In 1808, while living in Bamberg, he began his job as a theatre manager and a music critic, and Hoffman's break came a year later, with the publication of Ritter Gluck. The story centred on a man who meets, or thinks he has met, a long-dead composer, and played into the 'doppelgänger' theme – at that time very popular in literature. It was shortly after this that Hoffman began to use the pseudonym E. T. A. Hoffmann, declaring the 'A' to stand for 'Amadeus', as a tribute to the great composer, Mozart.

Over the next decade, while moving between Dresden, Leipzig and Berlin, Hoffman produced a great range of both literary and musical works. Probably Hoffman's most well-known story, produced in 1816, is 'The Nutcracker and the Mouse King', due to the fact that – some seventy-six years later - it inspired Tchaikovsky's ballet The Nutcracker.

In the same vein, his story 'The Sandman' provided both the inspiration for Léo Delibes's ballet Coppélia, and the basis for a highly influential essay by Sigmund Freud, called 'The Uncanny'. (Indeed, Freud referred to Hoffman as the "unrivalled master of the uncanny in literature.")

Alcohol abuse and syphilis eventually took a great toll on Hoffman though, and – having spent the last year of his life paralysed – he died in Berlin in 1822, aged just 46. His legacy is a powerful one, however: He is seen as a pioneer of both Romanticism and fantasy literature, and his novella, Mademoiselle de Scudéri: A Tale from the Times of Louis XIV is often cited as the first ever detective story.

The Stranger Child

Soon after those events, Felix and Christlieb had run off to the wood very early one morning. Their mother had impressed upon them that they were to be home very soon again, because it was necessary that they should stay in the house and read and write a great deal more than they used to do, that they might not lose countenance before the tutor, who was expected very soon. Wherefore Felix said, "We must jump and run about as much as we can for the little while that we are allowed to stay out here, that's all." So they immediately began to play at hare and hounds.

But that game, and also every other that they tried to play at, very soon only wearied them, and failed to amuse them after a second or two. They could not understand why it was that, on that particular day, thousands of vexatious annoyances should keep continually happening to them. The wind carried Felix's cap away into the bushes; he stumbled and fell down on his nose as he was running his best. Christlieb found herself hanging by her clothes in a thorn-tree, or banged her foot against a sharp stone, so that she had to shrink with pain. They soon gave it all up, and slunk along dejectedly through the wood.

"Let's go home," said Felix; "there's nothing else for it."

But instead of doing so, he threw himself down under a shady tree; Christlieb followed his example; and there the children lay, depressed and wretched, gazing at the ground.

7

"Ah!" said Christlieb; "if we only had our nice playthings."

"Bosh!" growled Felix; "what the better should we be? We should only smash them up and destroy them again. I'll tell you what it is, Christlieb. Mother is not far wrong, I suspect. The playthings were all right enough. But we didn't know how to play with them. And that's because we don't know anything about the 'sciences,' as they call them."

"You're quite right, Felix, dear," Christlieb said; "if we knew the 'sciences' all by heart, as those dressed-up cousins of ours do, we should still have your harp-man and your sportsman; and my poor doll would not be at the bottom of the duck-pond. Poor things that we are! Ah! we know nothing about the 'sciences'!"

And therewith Christlieb began to sob and cry bitterly, and Felix joined her in so doing. And they both howled and lamented till the wood re-echoed again, crying, "Poor unfortunate children that we are! we know nothing of the 'sciences.'"

But suddenly they ceased, and asked one another in amazement--

"Do you see, Christlieb?" "Do you hear, Felix?"

From out the deepest shades of the dark thicket which lay before the children, a wonderful luminousness began to shine, playing like moonlight over the leaves, which trembled in ecstasy. And through the whispering trees there came a sweet musical tone, like that which we hear when the wind awakens the chords slumbering within a harp. The children felt a sense of awe come over them. All their vexation had passed away from them; but tears of a sweet, unknown pain rose to their eyes.

As the radiance streamed brighter through the bushes, and the marvellous music-tones grew louder and louder, the children's hearts beat high: they gazed eagerly at the brightness, and then they saw, smiling at them from the thicket, the face of the most beautiful child imaginable, with the sun beaming on it in all its splendour.

"Oh, come to us!--come to us, darling child!" cried Christlieb and Felix, as they stretched their arms with indescribable longing towards the beautiful creature. "I am coming!--I am coming!" a sweet voice cried from the bushes; and then, as if borne on the wings of the morning breeze, the Stranger Child seemed to come hovering over to Christlieb and Felix.

HOW THE STRANGER CHILD PLAYED WITH FELIX AND CHRISTLIEB.

"I thought I heard you, out of the distance, crying and lamenting," said the Stranger Child, "and then I was very sorry for you. What is the matter, you dear children?--what is it you want?"

"Ah," Felix said, "we didn't quite know what it was that we did want! But now, as far as I can make out, what we wanted was just you yourself." "That is it!" Christlieb chimed in; "now that you are with us, we are happy again. Why were you so long in coming?"

In fact, both children felt as though they had known and played with the Stranger Child for a long time already, and that their unhappiness had been only because this beloved playmate was not with them.

"You see," Felix said, in continuation, "we really haven't got any playthings left; for I, like a stupid fool, went and destroyed a number of the very finest, which my cousin Pump-breeks gave me, and I shied them away. Never mind; we shall play somehow for all that."

"How can you talk so, Felix," said the Stranger Child, laughing aloud. "Certainly the stuff you threw away wasn't of much value; but you, and Christlieb too, are in the very middle of a quantity of the most exquisite play-things that were ever seen."

"Where--where are they?" Felix and Christlieb cried.

"Look round you," said the Stranger Child; and Felix and

Christlieb then saw how, out of the thick grass and the wool-like moss, all sorts of glorious flowers were peeping, with bright eyes gleaming, and between them many-coloured stones and crystalline shells sparkled and shone, while little golden insects danced up and down, humming little gentle songs.

"Now we will build a palace," said the Stranger Child. "Help me to get the stones together." And the Stranger stooped down and began choosing stones of pretty colours. Felix and Christlieb helped, and the Stranger Child knew so well how to set the stones up on one another that soon there arose tall columns, shining in the sun like polished metal, while an aerial golden roof vaulted itself over them at the top. Then the Stranger Child kissed the flowers which were peeping from the ground; when, with sweet whisperings, they shot up higher, and, embracing each other lovingly, formed sweet-scented arcades and covered walks, in which the children danced about, full of delight and gladness. The Stranger Child clapped hands; and then the golden roof of the palace, which was formed of insects' golden wings vaulted together, went asunder with a hum, and the pillars melted away into a plashing silver stream, on whose banks the varied flowers took up their stations, and peered inquiringly into its ripples, or, moving their heads from side to side, listened to its baby pattering. Then the Stranger Child plucked blades of grass, and gathered little twigs from trees, strewing them down before Felix and Christlieb. But those blades of grass presently turned into the prettiest little dolls ever seen;

11

and the twigs became delicious little huntsmen. The dolls danced round Christlieb; let her take them up in her lap, and whispered, in delicate little voices, "Be kind to us!--love us, dearest Christlieb!" The hunters shouted, "Halloa! halloa! the hunt's up!" and blew their horns, and bustled about. Then hares came darting out of the bushes, with dogs after them, and the hunters banging about. This was delightful.

Then all disappeared again. Christlieb and Felix cried, "What has become of the dolls? where are the hunters?" The Stranger Child said, "Oh, they are all at your disposal; they are close by you at any moment when you want them. But hadn't you rather come on through the wood a little now?" "Oh, yes! yes!" cried Felix and Christlieb. The Stranger Child took hold of their hands, crying, "Come; come!"

And with that they went off. But it could not be called "running," really, for the children floated along, lightly and easily, through amongst the trees, whilst all the bird's went fluttering along beside them, singing and warbling in the blithest fashion. All of a sudden up they soared, far into the sky. "Good morning, children! Good morning, Fritz, my crony!" cried the stork in the by-going.

"Don't hurt me! don't hurt me!" screamed the hawk. "I'm not going to touch your pigeons." And he swept away as hard as his long wings would carry him, alarmed at the children. Felix shouted with delight, but Christlieb was frightened. "Oh, my breath's going!" she cried; "I shall tumble!" And just at that moment the Stranger Child let them all three down to the ground again, and said: "Now I shall sing you

12

the Forest-Song, as a good-bye for to-day. I shall come again to-morrow." Then the Child took out a little horn, of which the golden windings looked almost as if made of wreaths of flowers, and began to sound it so beautifully that the whole wood echoed wondrously with the lovely music of it, whilst the nightingales (which had come up fluttering as if in answer to the horn's summons, and were sitting on the branches, as close as they could to the children) sang their sweetest songs. But all at once the music grew fainter and fainter, till nothing of it remained but a soft whisper, which seemed to come from the thicket into which the Stranger Child had disappeared. "To-morrow!--to-morrow I come again!" the children could just hear, as if from an immense distance. They could not give themselves any explanation of their feelings, for never, never had they known such happiness and enjoyment before in their lives.

"And, oh, I wish it were to-morrow now!" they both cried, as they hastened home as hard as they could, to tell their parents all that had happened to them.

WHAT BARON VON BRAKEL AND HIS LADY SAID, AND WHAT HAPPENED FURTHER.

"I could almost fancy the children had dreamt all this," the Baron said to his wife, when Felix and Christlieb, full of the Stranger Child, could not cease from talking of all that had happened--the delightsomeness of their new friend, the exquisite music, the wonderful events generally--"but then," said the Baron, "when I remember that they could not both have dreamt just the same things at the same time, really, when all's said and done, I cannot get to the bottom of it all."

"Don't trouble your head about it, dear," said Frau von Brakel. "My idea is that this Stranger Child was nobody but the schoolmaster's boy, Gottlieb, from the village. It must have been he that ran over, and put all this nonsense in the children's heads. We must take care that he is not allowed to do it any more."

The Baron, was by no means of his wife's opinion; and, with the view of getting better at the rights and wrongs of the affair, the children were brought in and made to describe minutely what the child was like; how it was dressed, and so forth. With respect to its appearance, both Felix and Christlieb agreed that its face was fair as the lilies; that it had cheeks like roses, cherry lips, bright blue eyes, locks of golden hair, and that it was more beautiful altogether than words could tell. As regarded its dress, all they knew was that it certainly had not a blue-striped jacket and trousers, or a black leather cap, such as the schoolmaster's Gottlieb wore. On the other hand, all they said of its dress sounded utterly fabulous and absurd. For Christlieb said its dress was wondrous beautiful, shining and gleaming, as if made of the petals of roses; whilst Felix maintained that it was sparkling golden green, like spring-leaves in the sunshine. Felix further said that the child could not possibly have any connection with such a person as a school master, because it was too deeply acquainted with sportsmanship and woodcraft, and must consequently belong to some very home and head-quarters of forest lore, and was going to be the grandest sportsman ever heard of. "Oh, Felix!" Christlieb broke in, "how can you say that dear little girl could ever be a sportsman? She may, perhaps, know a good deal about that too, but I'm sure she knows a great deal more about house-management; or how should she have dressed those dolls for me so beautifully, and made such delightful dishes?" Thus Felix thought the Stranger Child was a boy, and Christlieb, a girl; and those contradictory opinions could not be reconciled.

Fran von Brakel thought it was a pity to go into nonsense of this kind with children; but the Baron thought differently, and said: "I should only have to follow the children into the woods, to find out what wondrous sort of creature this is that comes to play with them; but I can't help feeling that if I did I should spoil what is for them a great pleasure; and for that reason I don't want to do it."

Next day, when Felix and Christlieb went off to the wood at the usual time, they found the Stranger Child waiting for them; and, if their play had been glorious on the former day, this day the Stranger Child did the most miraculous things imaginable, so that Felix and Christlieb shouted for rapture over and over again. It was delicious and most enjoyable that, during their play, the Stranger Child talked so prettily and comprehendingly with the trees, the bushes, the flowers, and the brook which ran through the wood, and they all answered so understandably that Felix and Christlieb knew everything that they said.

The Stranger Child said to the alder-thicket, "What is it that you black-looking folks are muttering and whispering to each other again?" and the branches took to shaking more forcibly, and they laughed and whispered "Ha, ha, ha! we are delighting ourselves over the charming things that friend Morning-breeze was saying to us when he came rustling over from the blue hills, in advance of the sunbeams. He brought us thousands of greetings and kisses from the Golden Queen; and plenty of wing-waftings, full of the sweetest perfume."

"Oh, silence!" the flowers broke in, interrupting the talk of the branches. "Hold your tongues on the score of that flatterer, who is so vain about the perfumes which his false caresses rob us of. Never mind the thickets, children; let them lisp and whisper; look at us--listen to us. We love you so, and we dress ourselves out, day by day, in the loveliest colours merely to give you pleasure."

"And do we not love you, you beautiful flowers?" said the Stranger Child. But Christlieb knelt down on the ground, and stretched out her arms, as if she would take all the beautiful flowers to her heart, crying, "Ah, I love you all, every one of you!" Felix cried, "I love you all, too, flowers, in your bright dresses. Still I dote upon green, and the woods, and the trees. The woods have to take care of you, and shelter you, bonny little things that you are."

Then came a sighing out of the tall, dark fir-trees; and they said, "That is very true, you clever boy; and you are not to be afraid of us, when our cousin, the storm, comes rushing at us, and we have to hold a rather strenuous bit of argument with that rough customer."

"All right," said Felix. "Groan, and sigh, and snarl as much as you like, you green giants that you are; then is when the real woodsman's heart begins to rejoice."

"You are quite right there," the forest brook plashed and rustled. "But what is the good of always hunting--always rushing in storm and turmoil? Come, and sit down nicely among the moss, and listen to me. I come from far-away places, out of a deep, dark, rocky cleft. I have delightful tales to tell you; and always something new, wave after wave, for ever and ever. And I will show you the loveliest pictures, if you will but look properly into this clear mirror of mine. Vaporous blue of the sky--golden clouds--bushes, flowers and trees, and your very selves, you beautiful children, I draw lovingly into the depths of my bosom."

"Felix and Christlieb," said the Stranger Child, looking round with wondrous blissfulness, "only listen how they all love us. But the redness of the evening is rising behind the hills, and the nightingale is calling me home."

"Oh, but let us just fly a little, as we did yesterday," Felix prayed.

"Yes," said Christlieb, "but not quite so high. It makes my head so giddy."

Then the Stranger Child took them by the hands again, and they went soaring up into the golden purple of the evening sky, while the birds crowded and sang round them. That was a shouting and a jubilating! In the shining clouds Felix saw, as if in wavering flame, beautiful castles all of rubies and other precious stones. "Look! look! Christlieb!" he cried, full of rapture, "look at all those splendid palaces! Let us fly along as fast as we can, and we shall get to them." Christlieb saw the castles too, and forgot her fear, as she was not looking down, this time, but up before her.

"Those are my beloved air-castles," the Stranger Child said. "But I don't think we shall get any further to-day.".

Felix and Christlieb seemed to be in a dream, and could not make out at all how they came to find themselves, presently, with their father and mother.

CONCERNING THE STRANGER CHILD'S HOME.

In the most beautiful part of the wood beside the brook, between whispering bushes, the Stranger Child had set up a most glorious tent, made of tall, slender lilies, glowing roses, and tulips of every hue; and beneath this tent Felix and Christlieb were sitting with the Stranger Child, listening to the forest-brook as it went on whispering the strangest things imaginable.

"I'll tell you, darling boy," Felix said, "I can't properly understand all that he, there, is saying; but I somehow feel that you could tell me, clearly and distinctly, what it is that he goes on murmuring. But most of all I should like you to tell me where it is that you come from, and where it is that you go away to, so fast, so fast, that we never can make out how you do it."

"Do you know, sweetest girl," said Christlieb, "our mother thinks you are the schoolmaster's boy, Gottlieb."

"Hold your tongue, stupid thing!" Felix cried. "Mother has never seen this darling boy, or she wouldn't have talked about the schoolmaster's Gottlieb. But come now, tell me where it is that you live, dear boy; fur we want to go and see you at your home in the winter time, when it storms and snows, and nobody can trace a track in the woods."

"Yes, yes!" said Christlieb. "Tell us, like a darling, where your home is; and all about your father and mother, and more than all, what your own name is."

The Stranger Child looked very thoughtfully at the sky, almost sorrowfully, and gave a deep sigh. Then, after some moments of silence, the Stranger Child said, "Ah, my dears, why must you ask about my home? Is it not enough for you that I come every day and play with you? I might tell you that my home lies behind those distant hills, which are like dim, jagged clouds. But though you were to travel day after day, for ever and ever, till you were standing on those hills, you would always see other, and other ranges of hills, further and further away, and my home would still be beyond them; and even if you reached them, you would still see others further away, and would have to go to them, and you would never come to where my home is."

"Ah me!" sighed Christlieb. "Then you must live hundreds and hundreds of miles away from us. It is only on a sort of visit that you are here?"

"Christlieb, darling," the Stranger Child said; "whenever you long for me with all your heart, I am with you immediately, bringing you all those plays and wonders from my home with me; and is not that quite as good as if we were in my home together, playing there?"

"Not at all," Felix said; "for I believe that your home is some most glorious place, full of all sorts of delightful things which you bring--some of them--here with you. I don't care how hard you may say the road is to your home, I mean to set out upon it this minute. To work one's way through forests-- by difficult tracks--to climb mountains, and wade rivers, and break through all sorts of thickets, and clamber over rugged rocks--all that is a woodsman's proper business, and I'm going to do it."

"And so you shall!" said the Stranger Child, smiling pleasantly; "for when you put it all so clearly before you, and make up your mind to it, it is as good as done. The land where I live is, in truth, so beautiful and glorious that I can give you no description of it. It is my mother who reigns over that country--all glory and loveliness--as queen."

"Ah, you are a prince!" "Ah, then, you are a princess! the two children cried together, amazed, and almost terrified.

"I am, certainly," the Stranger Child replied.

"Then you live in a beautiful palace?" Felix cried.

"Yes," said the Stranger Child. "My mother's palace is far more beautiful than those glittering castles which you saw in the evening clouds; for the gleaming pillars of her palace are all of the purest crystal, and they soar, slender and tall, into the blue of heaven; and upon them there rests a great, wide canopy; beneath that canopy sail the shining clouds, hither and thither, on golden wings, and the red of the evening and the morning rises and falls, and the sparkling stars dance in singing circles. Dearest playmates, you have heard of the fairies, who can bring about the most glorious wonders, as mortal men cannot; now, my mother is one of the most powerful fairies of all. All that lives and moves on earth she holds embraced to her heart in the purest and truest love; although, to her inward pain, many human beings will not allow themselves to come to any knowledge of her. But my mother loves children most of all; and thence

21

it is that the festivals which she holds in her kingdom for children are the most splendid and glorious of all. It is then that beautiful spirits belonging to my mother's kingdom, and to her royal palace, fly deftly through the sky, weaving and combining a shining rainbow, from one end of her palace to another, gleaming in the most brilliant dyes. Under those rainbows they build my mother's diamond throne, all of nothing but diamonds--diamonds which are, in appearance and in perfume, like lilies, roses, and carnations; and when my mother takes her place on her throne, the spirits play on their golden harps and their crystal cymbals, and to those instruments the court singers of her court sing with voices so marvellous, that one could die of rapture to hear them. Now, those singers are beautiful birds, bigger even than eagles, with feathers all purple-red, such as you have never seen the like of. And as soon as their music begins, everything in the palace, the woods, and the gardens moves and sings; and all around there are thousands of beautiful children in charming dresses, shouting and delighting. They chase each other amongst the bushes, and throw flowers at each other in play; they climb trees, where the winds swing them and rock them; they gather gold-glittering fruit, which tastes as nothing on earth does; and they play with tame deer and other charming creatures which come bounding up to them from among the trees; then they run up and down the rainbows, or they ride on the golden pheasants, which fly up among the gleaming clouds with them on their backs."

"How delightful that must be!" Christlieb and Felix cried

with rapture. "Oh, take us with you to your home! We want to stay there always!"

But the Stranger Child said, "I cannot take you with me to my home; it is too far away. You would have to be able to fly as far and as strongly as I can myself."

Felix and Christlieb were very sorry, and cast their eyes sadly down to the ground.

THE WICKED MINISTER AT THE FAIRY QUEEN'S COURT.

"And then," the Stranger Child continued, "you might not be as happy as you expect at my mother's court. Indeed, it might be a misfortune for you to go there. There are many children who cannot bear the singing of those purple-red birds, glorious as it is: it breaks their hearts, and they are obliged to die immediately. Others, who are too pert and adventurous in running up and down the rainbows, slip, and fall; and there are many who are so stupid and awkward, that they hurt the gold pheasants when they are riding on them. Then those birds, though they are good-tempered and kind-hearted, take this amiss, and they tear those children's breasts open with their sharp beaks, so that they fall down from the clouds bleeding. My mother is very very sorry when children come to misfortune in those ways, although it is all their own fault when they do. She would be only too happy if all the children in the world could enjoy the pleasures of her court and kingdom. But, although there are plenty who can fly strongly enough and far enough, they are often either too forward, or too timid, and cause her only sorrow and pain; and that is why she allows me to fly away from my home, and take to nice children all sorts of delightful playthings, as I have done to you."

"Ah," cried Christlieb, "I am sure I could never do anything to hurt those beautiful birds! But to run up and down a rainbow, that I am certain I never could. I shouldn't

24

like that."

"Now that would be just what I should delight in," Felix said; "and that is the very reason why I want to go and see your mother, the queen. Couldn't you bring one of those rainbows here with you?"

"No," the Stranger Child said, "I could not do that. And I must tell you that I have only been able to come to you by stealing away from home. Once on a time, I was quite safe every where, just as if I were at home, and my mother's beautiful kingdom seemed to extend all over the world; but now that a bitter enemy of hers, whom she has banished from her kingdom, is going raging about everywhere, I cannot be safe from being watched, pursued, and molested."

"Well," Felix cried, jumping up, and shieing the thorn-stick which he was cutting into the air, "I should like to come across the fellow who would do anything to harm you! He would have to do with me in the first place; and then I should send for father, and he would have him taken up and put in the tower."

"Ah," the Stranger Child said, "powerless as my bitter enemy is to harm me when I am at home, he is terribly dangerous when I am not there, and neither sticks nor prisons can protect me from him!"

"What sort of a nasty creature is it, then," Christlieb inquired, "that can do you so much harm?"

"I have told you that my mother is a mighty queen," the Stranger Child said; "and you know that queens, like kings, have courts and ministers belonging to them."

"Yes, yes," said Felix. "My own uncle, the count, is one of those ministers, and wears a star on his breast. Do your mother's ministers wear stars like him?"

"No," the Stranger Child said; "not exactly that; for most of them are shining stars themselves, and others of them do not wear any coats on which they could stick things of the sort. I must tell you that my mother's ministers are all powerful spirits, either hovering in the sky, or dwelling in the waters, doing, and carrying out everywhere what my mother orders them to do. Once, a long while ago, there came amongst us a stranger, who called himself Pepasilio, who said he was very learned, and could do more, and accomplish greater things, than all the others of us. My mother took him in amongst the ranks of her other ministers; but his natural spite and wickedness very soon developed themselves and came to light, Not only did he strive to undo all that the other ministers did, but he set himself specially to spoil all the happy enjoyments of children. He had pretended to the queen that he, of all others, was the very spirit who could make children glad, and happy, and clever; but instead of that, he hung himself with a weight of lead on to the tails of the pheasants, so that they could not fly aloft any more; and when the children climbed up the rose-trees, he would drag them down by the legs, so that they knocked their noses on the ground and made them bleed; and any that were jumping and dancing he dashed down to the ground, to go crawling wretchedly about there with downcast heads. Those who were singing he crammed all sorts of nasty stuff into the mouths of, so that they had to stop; for singing he could not abide. As for the poor tame beasts, he always wanted to eat them, instead of playing with them, for he said that was what they were meant for. The worst was, that with the help of his followers, he had a way of smearing all the beautiful, sparkling precious stones of the palace, the many-tinted glowing flowers, the roses and lilies, and even the shining rainbows, with a horrible black juice, so that all the glory and the beauty of them was gone, and everything became sorrowful and dead. And when he had accomplished this, he would out with a loud ringing laugh, and say that everything was now just as he wished it to be. But when, at last, he declared that he did not consider my mother to be queen at all, and that the rule really belonged to him alone,--and when he went hovering up in the shape of an enormous fly, with flashing eyes, and a great trunk, or snout, sticking out, all about my mother's throne, buzzing and humming in an abominable manner,--then she, and all the rest of her court, saw that this malignant minister, who had come amongst us under the fine name of Pepasilio, was none other than Pepser, the morose and gloomy King of the Gnomes. But he had foolishly overestimated his power, as well as the bravery of his followers. The ministers of the Air department surrounded the queen, and fanned perfumed breezes towards her, whilst the ministers of the Fire department rushed up and down in billows of flame, and the singers (whose bills had been cleaned out) chanted the most full-voiced choruses, so that the queen neither saw nor heard the ugly Pepser, neither could she be aware of his evil-smelling breath. Moreover, at that moment, the pheasant prince seized him with his glittering beak, and gripped him so strenuously that he screamed with agony and rage; and then the pheasant prince let him down to the earth from a height of three thousand ells, so that he could not stir hand or foot till his aunt, and crony, the great blue toad, took him on her back, and so carried him home. Five hundred fine sprightly children armed themselves with fly-flappers, with which they banged Pepser's horrible followers to death, when they were still swarming about intending to destroy all the beautiful flowers. Now, as soon as Pepser was gone, all the black juice which he had covered everything over with, flowed away of itself, and everything was restored, and was soon beaming and shining, and blooming as gloriously as ever. You may imagine that this horrid Pepser has no more power in my mother's kingdom. But he knows that I often venture out, and he follows me everywhere, in shapes of every kind, so that, wretched child that I am, I often do not know where to hide myself in my flight; and that is why I often get away from you so quickly that you cannot see what becomes of me. Therefore things must go on just as they are; and I can assure you that if I were to try to take you with me to my home, Pepser would be sure to lie in wait for us, and kill us."

Christlieb wept bitterly over the danger to which the Stranger Child must always be exposed. But Felix said, "If that horrible Pepser is nothing but a great fly, I'll soon be at him with father's big fly-flapper; and if once I give him a good crack on the nose with it, Aunty Toad will have a job to get him home, I can tell her."

HOW THE TUTOR ARRIVED, AND HOW THE CHILDREN WERE AFRAID OF HIM.

Felix and Christlieb ran home as fast as they could, crying, as they went, "Ah! the Stranger Child is a beautiful prince!"--"Ah! the Stranger Child is a beautiful princess!" They wanted, in their delight, to tell this to their parents; but they stood at the door like marble statues when they found the baron meeting them there with a stranger at his side, an extraordinary-looking personage, who muttered to himself, half intelligibly, "Ah, a nice pair of gawkies those are, it seems to me!"

The baron took him by the hand, saying, "This gentleman is the tutor whom your gracious uncle has sent. So say, 'How-do-you do, sir?' to him properly."

But the children looked askance at the man, and could move neither hand nor foot. This was because they had never seen such an extraordinary-looking creature. He was scarcely more than half a head taller than Felix; but he was stumpy and thick-set, and his little weasened legs formed an astonishing contrast with his body, which was stout and powerful. His shapeless head was almost to be called four-square, and his face was almost too ugly altogether. For not only was his nose much too long and sharp-pointed to suit with his fat, brownish cheeks, and his wide mouth, but his little prominent eyes glittered so alarmingly that one hardly liked to look at him. Moreover, he had a black periwig crammed on to his four-cornered head; he was clad in black from top to toe, and his name was "Tutor Ink."

Now, as the children stood staring like stone images, their mother got angry, and cried, "Good gracious, children, what are you thinking of? This gentleman will take you for a pair of raw country gabies! Come, come; give him your hands!"

The children, taking heart of grace, did as their mother bade them. But as soon as the tutor took hold of their hands, they jumped back with a loud cry of "Oh! oh! It hurts!" The tutor laughed aloud, and showed a needle which he had hidden in his hand, to prick the children with. Christlieb was weeping; but Felix growled, in an aside, "Just you try that again, little Big-belly!"

"Why did you do that, dear Mr. Tutor Ink?" the baron asked, rather annoyed.

The tutor answered, "Well, it is my way; I can't alter it!" With which he stuck his hands in his sides, and went on laughing, till at length his laughter sounded as ugly as the noise of a broken rattle.

"You seem to be a person fond of your little jokes, Master Tutor Ink!" the baron said. But he, and his wife, and most particularly the children, were beginning to feel very eery and uncomfortable. "Well, well," said Tutor Ink, "what sort of a state are these little crabs here in? Pretty well grounded in the sciences? We'll see directly." With which he began to ask questions of Felix and Christlieb, of the sort that their uncle and aunt had asked of their cousins. But, as they both declared that, as yet, they did not know any of the sciences, by heart, Tutor Ink beat his hands over his head till everything rang again, and cried, like a man possessed, "A pretty story indeed! No sciences! Then we've got our work cut out for us. However, we shall soon make a job of it."

Felix and Christlieb could both write fairly well, and, from many old books which their father put in their hands, and which they were fond of reading, they had learned a good many pretty stories, and could repeat them. But Tutor Ink despised all this, and said it was stupid nonsense.

Alas! there was no more running about in the woods to be so much as thought of. Instead of that, the children had to sit within the four walls of the house all day long, and babble, after Tutor Ink, things which they did not in the least understand. It was really a heart-breaking business. With what longing eyes they looked at the woods! Often it was as if they heard, amidst the happy songs of the birds, and the rustling of the trees, the Stranger Child's voice calling to them and saying, "Felix! Christlieb! are you not coming any more to play with me? Oh, come! I have made you a palace, all of flowers; we will sit there, and I will give you all sorts of beautiful stones, and then we'll soar into the air, and build ourselves cloud-castles. Come! oh come!"

At this, the children were drawn to the woods with all their thoughts, and neither saw nor heard their tutor any longer. But he would get very angry, thump on the table with both his fists, and hum, and growl, and snarl, "Pim--sim--prr--srr knurr kirr--what's all this? Wait a little! "Felix, however, did not endure this very long; he jumped up, and cried, "Don't bother me with your stupid nonsense,

Mr. Ink; I must be off to the woods! Go and get hold of Cousin Pumpbreeks; that's the sort of stuff for him. Come along, Christlieb! The Stranger Child is waiting for us;" with which they started off. But Tutor Ink sprang after them with remarkable agility, and seized hold of them just outside the door. Felix fought like a man, and Tutor Ink was on the point of getting the worst of it, as the faithful Sultan came to Felix's help. Sultan--generally a good, kindly-behaved dog took a strong dislike to Tutor Ink the moment he set eyes on him. Whenever the tutor came near him, he growled, and swept about him so forcibly with his tail that he nearly knocked the tutor down, managing deftly to hit him great thumps on his little weazened legs. So Sultan came dashing up, when Felix was holding the tutor by the shoulders, and hung on to his coat-tails. Master Ink raised a doleful yell, which brought up the baron to the rescue. The tutor let go his hold of Felix, and Sultan let go his hold on the tutor's coat-tails.

"He said we weren't to go to the woods any more," cried Christlieb, weeping and lamenting. And although the baron gave Felix a good scolding, he was very sorry that the children might not go wandering, as they used, amongst the trees and bushes, and told the tutor that he wished him to go with them into the woods for a certain time every day.

The tutor did not like the idea at all. He said, "Ah, Herr Baron, if you had but a sensible piece of garden, with nicely-clipped box, and railed-in enclosures, one might go and take the children for a little walk there of forenoons! But what in all the world is the good of going into a wild forest?"

32

The children did not like it either, saying, "What business has Tutor Ink in our darling wood?"

HOW TUTOR INK TOOK THE CHILDREN FOR A WALK IN THE WOODS, AND WHAT HAPPENED ON THE OCCASION.

"Well, Master Ink, isn't it delightful in our wood here?" Felix said, as they were making their way through the rustling thickets. Tutor Ink made a face, and answered, "Stupid nonsense! There's no road. All that one does is to tear one's stockings. And one can't say or hear a word of sense, for the abominable screaming noise the birds are making."

"Ha, ha! master," said Felix, "I see you don't know anything about singing! And I daresay you don't hear when the morning wind is talking with the bushes, and the old forest brook is telling all those delightful tales." "And you don't even love the flowers," Christlieb chimed in; "do you, master?"

At this the tutor's face became of even a deeper cherry-brown than it was usually; and he beat with his hands about him, crying, "What stupid, ridiculous nonsense you are talking! Who has put such trash in your heads? Who ever heard that woods and streams had got the length of engaging in rational conversation? Neither is there anything in the chirping of birds. I like flowers well enough when they are nicely arranged in a room in glasses. They smell then; and one doesn't require a scent-bottle. But there are no proper flowers in woods."

"But don't you see those dear little lilies of the valley, peeping up at you with such bright, loving eyes?" Christlieb said.

"What? what?" the tutor screamed. "Flowers--eyes? Ha, ha! Nice 'eyes' indeed! The useless things haven't even got what you would call a smell!" With which Master Ink bent down and plucked up a handful of them, roots and all, and chucked them away into the thickets. To the children it seemed, almost, as if they heard a cry of pain pass through the wood. Christlieb could not help bitter tears, and Felix gnashed his teeth in anger. Just then, a little siskin went fluttering close past the tutor's nose, alighted on a branch, and began a joyous song. "That is a mockingbird, I think!" said the tutor; and, taking up a stone, he threw it at the poor bird, which it struck, and silenced into death; it fell from the green branch to the ground.

Felix could restrain himself no longer. "You horrible Tutor Ink," he cried, "what had the bird done to you that you should strike it dead? Ah, where are you, you beautiful Stranger Child? Oh come! only come! Let us fly far, far away. I cannot stay beside this horrible creature any longer. I want to go to your home with you." Christlieb chimed in, sobbing and weeping bitterly, crying, "Oh, thou darling child, come to us, come to us! Rescue us, rescue us! Tutor Ink is killing us, as he is killing the flowers and the birds."

"What do you mean by the Stranger Child?" Tutor Ink asked. But at that instant there came a louder whispering and rustling amongst the bushes, mingled with melancholy, heart-breaking tones, as if of muffled bells tolling in the far distance. In a shining cloud, which came sailing over above them, they saw the beautiful face of the Stranger Child, and presently it came wholly into view, wringing its little hands, whilst tears, like glittering pearls streamed down its rosy cheeks. "Ah, darling playmates," cried the Stranger Child, in tones of sorrow, "I cannot come to you any more. You will never see me again. Farewell, farewell! The gnome Pepser has you in his power. Oh, you poor children, good-bye, good-bye!" and the Stranger Child soared up far into the sky. But, at the children's backs, there began a horrid, fearsome sort of buzzing and humming, and snarling and growling; and lo! Tutor Ink had taken the shape of an enormous frightful-looking fly. And the horrible part of the thing was, that he had a man's face at the same time, and even some of his clothes on still. He began to fly upwards, slowly and with difficulty, evidently with the intention of following the Stranger Child. Felix and Christlieb, overpowered with terror, ran away out of the wood as quickly as they could, and did not so much as dare to look up to the sky till they had got some distance off. When they did so, they could just perceive a shining speck in the sky, glittering amongst the clouds like a star, and apparently coming nearer, and downwards. "That's the Stranger Child," Christlieb cried. The star grew bigger and bigger, and as it did, they could hear a braying of trumpets; and presently they saw that the star was a splendid bird, with wondrous shining plumage, coming soaring down to the wood, flapping its mighty wings, and singing loud and clear. "Ha!" cried Felix, "this is the pheasant prince. He will bite Master Tutor Ink to death. The Stranger Child is saved and

36

so are we! Come, Christlieb; let us get home as fast as we can, and tell father all about it."

HOW THE BARON TURNED TUTOR INK OUT OF DOORS.

The baron and his spouse were both sitting before the door of their simple dwelling, looking at the evening-red, which was beginning to flame up from behind the blue mountains in golden streamers. They had their supper laid out on a little table: it consisted of a noble jug of splendid milk, and a plate of bread-and-butter.

"I don't know," the baron began, "where Tutor Ink can be staying out so long with the children. At first there was no getting him to go out at all to the wood, and now there's no getting him back from it. He's really a very extraordinary fellow, this Tutor Ink, taking him all in all. I sometimes almost wish he had never entered our doors. To begin with, his pricking the children with that needle was a thing that I cannot say I liked; and I don't think his knowledge of the sciences amounts to very much, either. He plappers out a lot of stuff that nobody run make head or tail of, and can tell you what kind of spatterdashes the Grand Mogul puts on; but when he goes outside, he can't tell a lime-tree from a chestnut; and his behaviour has always struck me as being most remarkable."

"I feel just as you do, dearest husband," said Frau von Brakel; "and, glad as I was that your great cousin should interest himself about the children, I feel quite sure, now, that he might have done it in other and better ways than by saddling us with this Tutor Ink. As regards his knowledge of the sciences, I don't pretend to give an opinion; but I know that the little black creature, with his little weeny legs, is more and more disagreeable to me every day. He has such a nasty way of gobbling things. He can't see a drop of beer at the bottom of a glass, or the fag-end of a jug of milk, but he must gulp them down his throat; and if he finds the sugar-box open, he's at it in a moment, snuffing at the sugar, and dipping his fingers in it, till one has to clap to the lid in his face; and then away he darts, humming and buzzing in a way that's most disgusting and abominable."

The baron was going to carry this conversation further, when Felix and Christlieb came running home through amongst the birches.

"Hurrah! hurrah!" Felix kept shouting, "the pheasant prince has bitten Master Tutor Ink to death!"

"Oh, mamma dear," cried Christlieb, "Master Tutor Ink is not a Tutor Ink at all! What he really is, is Pepser, king of the Gnomes; a great, monstrous fly, but a fly with a wig on, and shoes and stockings!"

The parents gazed at the children in utter amazement, as they went on excitedly telling them all about the Stranger Child, whose mother was a great fairy queen; and of the Gnome King Pepser, and his combat with the pheasant prince.

"Who on earth has been cramming all this nonsense into your heads?" the baron asked over and over again. "Have you been dreaming? or what in the name of goodness has happened to you?" However, the children declared, and stuck to it, that everything had happened just as they told it, and that the horrible Pepser, who had given himself out as being Master Ink, the tutor, must be lying killed in the wood.

Frau von Brakel struck her hands over her head and cried, in much sorrow, "Oh, children, children, I don't know what on earth is to become of you, when fearful things of this sort come into your heads, and you won't let yourselves be persuaded to the contrary!"

But the baron grew very grave and thoughtful. "Felix," he said, "you are really a very sensible boy now; and I must admit that Tutor Ink has always, from the very first, struck me as being a very strange, mysterious creature. Indeed, it often seemed to me that there was something very queer about him, which I could by no means get to the bottom of; he is not like the common run of tutors at all. Your mother and I are by no means satisfied with him, particularly your mother. He has such a terribly liquorish tooth of his own, there's no keeping him away from sweet things! And then he hums and buzzes in such a distressing way! Altogether, I can assure you he wouldn't have been here much longer. No! But now, my dear boy, just bethink yourself calmly; even if there were, really, any such nasty things as gnomes existing in the world, could (I ask you now to think it over calmly and rationally), could, I say, a tutor really be a fly?"

Felix looked his father steadily in the face with his clear blue eyes, as he repeated this question. "Well," said Felix, "I never thought very much about that; in fact, I should not have believed it myself, if the Stranger Child had not said so, and if I had not seen, with my own eyes, that he is a horrible, nasty fly, and only pretends to be Tutor Ink. And then," continued Felix, while the baron shook his head in silence, like one who does not know quite what to say, or think, "see what mother says about his fondness for sweet things. Isn't that just like a fly? Flies are always grabbing at sweet things. And then, his hummings and buzzings!"

"Silence!" cried the baron. "Whatever Tutor Ink may really be, one thing is certain; that the pheasant prince has not bitten him to death, for here he comes out of the wood!"

At this the children uttered loud screams, and fled into the house.

For, in truth, Tutor Ink was approaching out of the wood, up the path among the birches. But he was all wild-looking and bewildered, with sparkling eyes, and his wig all touzled. He was buzzing and humming, and making great springs, high off the ground, first to one side, then to another, banging his head against the birches till you heard them resound. When he got to the house, he dashed at the milk-jug and popped his face into it, so that the milk ran over the sides; and he gulped it down, making a horrible noise of swallowing.

"For the love of heaven, Master Ink," cried Fran von Brakel, "what are you about?"

"Are you out of your senses?" said the baron. "Is the foul fiend after you?"

But, regardless of those interrogations, Master Ink, taking his mouth from the milk-jug, threw himself down bodily on the dish of bread-and-butter; fluttered over it with his coat-tails, and, somehow, made such play over it with his weazened legs, that he smoothed it down all over. Then, with a louder buzzing, he made for the house-door; but he couldn't manage to get into the house, but staggered hither and thither as if he was drunk, banging against the windows till they rattled and rang.

"I'll tell you what it is, my good sir!" cried the baron. "This is pretty behaviour! Look out, or you'll come to grief before you know where you are!" And he tried to seize Master Ink by the coat-tails; but Master Ink always managed to elude him, deftly. Here Felix came running out, with his father's big fly-flapper in his hand; and he gave it to the baron, crying, "Here you are, father; knock the horrible Pepser to death!"

The baron took the fly-flapper, and then they all set to work at Master Ink. Felix, Christlieb, and their mother took table-napkins, and made sweeps with them in the air, driving the tutor backwards and forwards, here and there; whilst the baron kept letting drive at him with the fly-flapper, which did not hit him, unfortunately, because he took good care never to stay a moment in the same place. And wilder and wilder grew the chase. "Summ-summ----simm-simm----trr-trr," went the tutor, storming hither and thither; "huss-huss," went the table-napkins, pursuing the foe; "klip-klap" fell the baron's strokes with the flapper, thick as hail. At last the baron managed to hit the tutor's coat-tails; he fell down with a groan. But just as the baron was going to get a second stroke at him, he bounced up into the air, with renewed and

42

redoubled strength, stormed, humming and buzzing, away through the birches, and was seen no more.

"A good job," said the baron, "that we're well rid of horrible Tutor Ink: never shall he cross my threshold again."

"No; that he shall not!" said Frau von Brakel. "Tutors with such objectionable manners can do nothing but mischief, when just the contrary ought to be the case. Brags about his 'sciences,' and then goes flop into the milk-jug. A nice sort of a tutor, upon my word!"

But the children laughed and shouted, crying, "Hip-hip, hurrah! It's all right now! Father has hit Tutor Ink a good one on the nose, and we've got rid of him for good and all."

THAT WHICH CAME TO PASS IN THE WOOD, AFTER TUTOR INK WAS GOT RID OF.

Felix and Christlieb breathed freely again now. A great weight was taken off their hearts. Above all things, there was the delicious thought that, now that the horrid Pepser was gone, the Stranger Child would be sure to come back, and play with them as of yore. They hurried into the wood, full of sweet hope and happy expectancy. But everything there was silent and desolate. Not a merry note of finch or siskin was to be heard; and in place of the gladsome rustling of the bushes and the joyous voice of the brook, sighs of sorrow seemed to be passing through the air, and the sun cast only faint and feeble glimpses through the clouded sky. Presently great dark clouds began to pile themselves up; thunder muttered in the distance; a storm-wind howled, and the tall fir-trees creaked and groaned. Christlieb clung to Felix, in alarm. But he said, "What's come to you? What are you afraid of? There's going to be a thunderstorm. We must get home as fast as we can; that's all!"

So they set off to do so; but somehow--they didn't know why--instead of getting out of the wood, they seemed to keep getting farther and farther into it. The darkness deepened: great rain-drops fell, faster and faster, thicker and thicker, and flashes of lightning darted hither and thither, hissing as they passed. The children came to a stand by the edge of an impassable thicket. "Let's duck down here for a little, Christlieb," said Felix; "the storm won't last long." Christlieb was crying from fear, but she did as Felix asked her. Scarcely had they sat down among the thick bushes, however, when nasty, snarling voices began to speak, behind them, saying:

"Stupid things! Senseless creatures! You despised us; didn't know how to treat us--what to do with us. So now you can do your best without any playthings, senseless creatures that you are!" Felix looked round, and felt very eery and uncomfortable when he saw the sportsman and the harper rise up out of the thicket into which he had thrown them, staring at him with dead eyes and struggling and fighting about them with their hands. Moreover, the harper twanged on his strings so that they gave out a horrible, nasty, eery clinkering and rattling; and the sportsman went so far as to take a deliberate aim at Felix with his gun; and both of them croaked out, "Wait a little, you boy and you girl. We are obedient pupils of Master Tutor Ink: he'll be here directly, and then we'll pay you out nicely for despising us." Terrified--regardless of the rain, which was now streaming in torrents, and of the rattling peals of thunder, and the gale which was roaring through the firs--the children ran away from thence, and came to the brink of the pond which bordered the wood. But as soon as they got there, lo and behold! Christlieb's big doll, which Felix had thrown into the water, rose out of the sedges, and squeaked out, in a horrible voice, "Wait a little, you boy and you girl! Stupid things! Senseless creatures! You despised me; didn't know what to do with me--how to treat me. So now you can get on without playthings the best way you can. I am an obedient pupil of Master Tutor Ink's:

he'll be here directly, and then you'll be nicely paid out for despising me." And then the nasty thing sent great splashes of water flying at Felix and Christlieb, though they were wet through already with the rain.

Felix could not endure this terrible process of haunting. Poor Christlieb was half dead, so they ran off again, as hard as they could; but soon, in the heart of the wood, they sank down, exhausted with weariness and terror. Then they heard a humming and a buzzing behind them. "Oh, heavens!" cried Felix; "here comes Tutor Ink, now!" At that moment his consciousness left him, and so did Christlieb's too.

When they came back to their senses, they found themselves lying on a bed of soft moss. The storm was over, the sun was shining bright and kindly, and the raindrops were hanging on the glittering bushes and trees like sparkling jewels. The children were much surprised to find that their clothes were quite dry, and that they felt no trace of either cold or wet. "Ah!" cried Felix, stretching his arms to the sky; "the Stranger Child must have protected us." And then they both called out so loud that the wood re-echoed: "Ah, thou darling child, do but come to us again! We do so long for you; we cannot live without you!" And it seemed, too, as though a bright beam of light came darting through the trees, making the flowers lift up their heads as it touched them. But though the children called upon their playfellow yet more movingly, nothing made itself seen. They crept home in silence and sadness. But their parents were very glad to see them, having been exceedingly anxious about them during the storm. The baron said, "It is a good thing that you are home again; for I confess I was afraid that Tutor Ink was still hanging about somewhere in the wood, and on your track."

Felix related all that had happened in the wood. "That is all stupid nonsense," their mother said. "If you are to go dreaming all that sort of stuff in the wood, you shan't be allowed to go there any more. You'll have to stop at home." And indeed--although, when they begged that they might be allowed to go back there, their mother yielded--it so came about that they didn't care very much about doing it. Alas! the Stranger Child was never there; and whenever they got far into the wood, or reached the bank of the pond, they were jeered at by the harper, the sportsman, and the doll, who cried to them, "Stupid things! Senseless creatures! You must do without playthings. You didn't know how to treat us clever, cultivated people--stupid things, senseless creatures that you are!"

This being unendurable, the children preferred staying at home.

CONCLUSION.

"I don't know," said the baron to his lady one day, "what it is that has been the matter with me for the last few days. I feel so queer and so odd, that I could almost fancy Tutor Ink has put some spell upon me. Ever since the moment when I hit him that crack with the fly-flapper, all my limbs have felt like bits of lead."

And the baron did really grow weaker and paler, day by day. He gave up walking about his grounds; he no longer went bustling about the house, cheerily ordering matters as he used to do; he sat, hour after hour, in deep meditation, and would get Felix and Christlieb to repeat to him, over and over again, all about the Stranger Child; and when they spoke eagerly of all the marvels connected with the Stranger Child, and of the beautiful brilliant kingdom which was its home, he would give a melancholy smile, and the tears would come to his eyes.

But Felix and Christlieb could not reconcile themselves to the circumstance that the Stranger Child went on keeping aloof from them, leaving them exposed to the nasty behaviour of those troublesome puppets in the thicket and the duck pond, on account of which they did not like now to frequent the wood at all.

But one morning, when it was fine and beautiful, the baron said, "Come along, children; we'll go to the wood together, you and I. Master Ink's nasty pupils shan't do you any harm." So he took them by the hands, and they all three went together to the wood, which that day was fuller than ever of bright sunshine, perfume, and song. When they had laid themselves down amongst the tender grass, and the sweet-scented flowers, the baron began as follows:--

"You dear children, I have for some time had a great longing to tell you a thing, and I cannot delay doing so any longer. It is, that--once on a time--I knew the beautiful Stranger Child that used to show you such lovely things in the wood, just as well as you did yourselves. When I was about your age, that child used to come to me too, and play with me in the most wonderful way. How it was that it came to leave me, I cannot quite remember; and I don't understand how I had so completely forgotten all about it till you spoke to me about what had happened to you, and then I didn't believe you, though I often had a sort of dim consciousness that what you told me was the truth. But within the last few days, I have been remembering and thinking about the delightful days of my own boyhood, in a way that I have not been able to do for many a long year. And then that beautiful magic-child came back to my memory, bright and glorious, as you saw it yourselves; and the same longing which filled your breasts came to mine too. But it is breaking my heart! I feel, and I know quite well, that this is the last time that I shall ever sit beneath these bonnie trees and bushes. I am going to leave you very soon, and when I am dead and gone, you must cling fast to that beautiful child."

Felix and Christlieb were beside themselves with grief and sorrow. They wept and lamented, crying, "No, no, father;

you are not going to die! You have many a long year to be with us still, and to play with the Stranger Child along with us."

But the next day, the baron lay sick in his bed. A tall, meagre man came and felt his pulse, and said, "You'll soon be better!" But he was not soon better. On the third day, the Baron von Brakel was no more. Ah, how Frau von Brakel mourned! How the children wrung their hands and cried, "Oh, father! our dear, dear father!"

Soon, when four peasants of Brakelheim had borne their master to his grave, there came to the house some horrible fellows, almost like Tutor Ink in appearance, and they told Frau von Brakel that they must take possession of all the piece of land, and the house, and everything in it, because the deceased baron owed all that, and more besides, to his cousin, who could wait no longer for his money. So that Frau von Brakel was a beggar, and had to go away from the pretty little village of Brakelheim, where she had spent so many happy years, and go to live with a relation not very far away. She and the children had to pack up whatever little bits of clothes and effects they had left, and with many tears take their leave, and set forth upon their way. As they crossed the bridge, and heard the loud voice of the forest stream, Frau von Brakel fell down in a swoon, and Felix and Christlieb sank on their knees beside her, and cried, with many sobs and tears, "Oh, unfortunate creatures that we are! Will no one take any pity on us?"

At that moment the distant rushing of the forest stream

seemed to turn into beautiful music. The thickets gave forth mysterious sighs, and presently all the forest streamed with wonderful, sparkling fires. And lo! the Stranger Child appeared, coming forth out of the sweet-smelling leafage, surrounded by such a brilliant light and radiance, that Felix and Christlieb had to shut their eyes at the brightness of it. Then they felt themselves gently touched, and the Stranger Child's beautiful voice said, "Oh, do not mourn so, dear playmates of mine! Do I not love you as much as ever? Can I ever leave you? No, no! Although you do not see me with your bodily eyes, I am always with you and about you, helping you with all my power to be always happy and fortunate. Only keep me in your hearts, as you have done hitherto, and neither the wicked Pepser, nor any other adversary, will have power to harm you. Only go on loving me truly and faithfully."

"Oh, that we shall--that we shall!" the children cried. "We love you with all our souls!"

When they were able to open their eyes again, the Stranger Child had vanished; but all their pain was gone from them, and they felt that a heavenly joy and gladness had arisen within their hearts. Frau von Brakel recovered slowly from her swoon, and said, "Children, I saw you in a dream. You seemed to be standing in a blaze of gleaming gold, and the sight has strengthened and refreshed me in a wonderful way."

Delight beamed in the children's eyes, and shone in their cheeks. They related how the Stranger Child had come to

51

them and comforted them. And their mother said, "I do not know how it is that I feel compelled to believe in this story of yours to-day, nor how my believing in it seems to have taken away all my sorrow and anxiety. Let us go on our way with confidence."

They were kindly received and welcomed by their relatives, and all that the Stranger Child promised came to pass. Whatever Felix and Christlieb undertook was sure to prosper, and they and their mother became quite happy. And, as their lives went on, they still, in dreams, played with the Stranger Child, which, never ceased to bring to them the loveliest wonders from its fairy home.

"No doubt," said Ottmar, when Lothair had finished, "your 'Stranger Child' is more purely a story for children than your 'Nutcracker.' Still, pardon me for saying so, you haven't been able to refrain from introducing a certain number of your confounded flourishes, such as no child could see to the bottom of."

"I," said Sylvester, "have long been acquainted with the little Devilkin that sits on Lothair's shoulder like a tame squirrel. He can't shut his ears to the strange things which the creature whispers to him."

"At all events," said Cyprian, "he ought to call those stories, 'Tales for Children, great and small,' instead of 'Tales for Children.'"

"Or," added Vincent, "'Tales for Children, and those who are not children.' In this way the entire world would be able to take them up and form their own opinion of them."

They all laughed, and Lothair, in comic anger, declared that in his next he would give full rein to his inspiration, regardless of consequences.

Midnight having struck, the friends said good-night, and separated in the happiest of moods.

www.ingramcontent.com/pod-product-compliance
Lightning Source LLC
Chambersburg PA
CBHW030542180626
46810CB00005B/1978